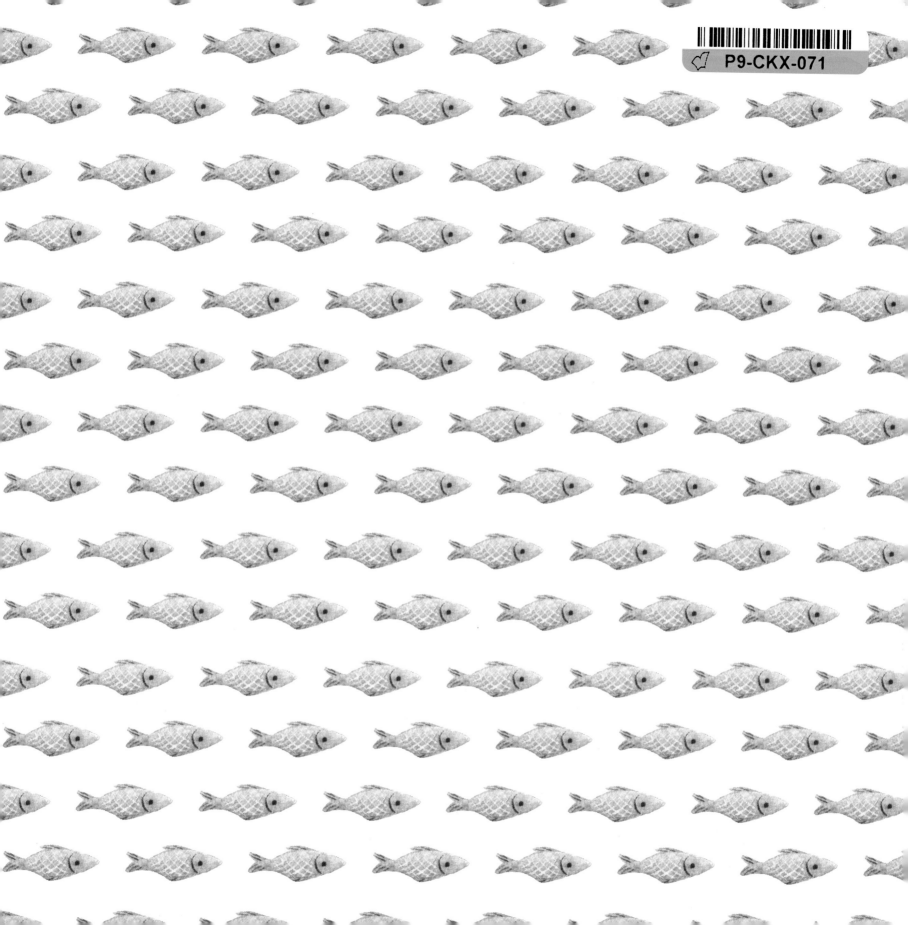

WHERE THE HEART IS

IRMA GOLD and SUSANNAH CRISPE

For the Frav crew – Thomas,
Hazel, Noah, Pippin, Harvey,
Vera and Oliver – with big love.
– I.G.

For everyone who helped me on
this adventure, and for Jeremy
and all his future adventures.
– S.C.

First published 2021

EK Books
an imprint of Exisle Publishing Pty Ltd
PO Box 864, Chatswood, NSW 2057, Australia
226 High Street, Dunedin, 9016, New Zealand
www.ekbooks.org

A CiP record for this book is available from the National Library
of Australia.

ISBN 978-1-925820-87-4

Designed by Mark Thacker
Typeset in Minya Nouvelle 17 on 25pt
Printed in China

This book uses paper sourced under ISO 14001 guidelines from
well-managed forests and other controlled sources.

10 9 8 7 6 5 4 3

Note on pronunciation:
If you'd like to know how to accurately pronounce
Joao and Dindim's names, head to Google!

In 2011, Dindim, a Magellanic penguin, washed up on an island village beach just outside Rio de Janeiro, Brazil, near Joao's home. Since his rescue, Dindim has spent eight months of every year with Joao, leaving in February for the Patagonia coasts of Argentina and Chile, and returning in June. The trip back to Joao is an extraordinary 8000 kilometres (4970 miles). Scientists say they have never seen anything like it. This true story inspired *Where the Heart Is.*

SOUTH AMERICA

PACIFIC OCEAN

ATLANTIC OCEAN

← Joao's Island

← Patagonia

On a beach in Brazil a tiny penguin was washed ashore. He was covered in oil and so sick that he couldn't open his eyes.

Old Joao found him and took him home. There he wiped the sticky oil from the penguin's feathers and fed him sardines.

He named him Dindim.

Every day Joao fed him sardines, and
after a week Dindim was strong again.
Joao took him down to the beach
to say goodbye.

But Dindim didn't want to leave.

Joao didn't want Dindim to leave
either, but he knew that it was the way
it must be. So he put Dindim in his
boat and rowed out to sea. The old man
tipped the penguin into the ocean, and
sadly rowed back to shore.

But as Joao walked up the sandy path to his shanty, there was Dindim, waiting. He had beaten the old man home. Dindim flapped his wings in welcome. Joao roared with laughter.

And so Dindim stayed.
The old man and the penguin
did everything together.

They ate sardine
sandwiches together.

They mended fishing
nets together.

They even did the shopping together.

But the best times were when Dindim lay in Joao's lap and sang to him, a lullaby of belonging.

Almost a year after he first arrived on
Joao's beach, Dindim shed his feathers and
grew in a new coat. He was becoming
a very handsome penguin indeed.

There came a day when Dindim knew in his
heart it was time to leave. He waddled down
to the water, honking a farewell.

Watching him go,
Joao's heart trembled.

Dindim swam for many days and nights,
barely stopping to sleep or eat.

He passed whales spouting
umbrellas, and albatross with
wings as big as waves.

When he reached the Patagonia
coast there was a whole beach
of new friends waiting.

Together they played in the inky ocean ...

whooshing through water and chasing fields of fish.

Dindim grew good and fat.

But sometimes, even when Dindim
was surrounded by his friends, he
felt lonely. There was an ache in his
heart, for he missed the old man.

After months in Patagonia, he could stay no longer. The thought of Joao tugged him back into the ocean.

He swam for many days and nights, all the way ...

hoping, hoping, hoping that the old man would be there to meet him.

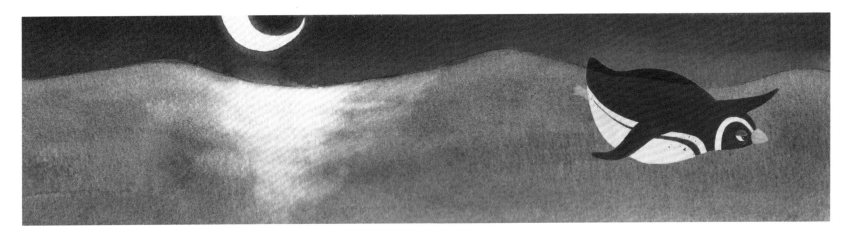

That he hadn't forgotten him.

Not far from Joao's beach, the sky
swelled and lightning jagged. Dindim
rode waves and wondered if he would
make it. He was exhausted.

A sea lion loomed out of the darkness,
her teeth scraping the tip of Dindim's tail.
Dindim darted left and right, pushing himself
as fast as his tired flippers would go.

He made it to the beach
but the sea lion lumbered after him.
Dindim could hear the slap of her
body and smell her terrible breath.

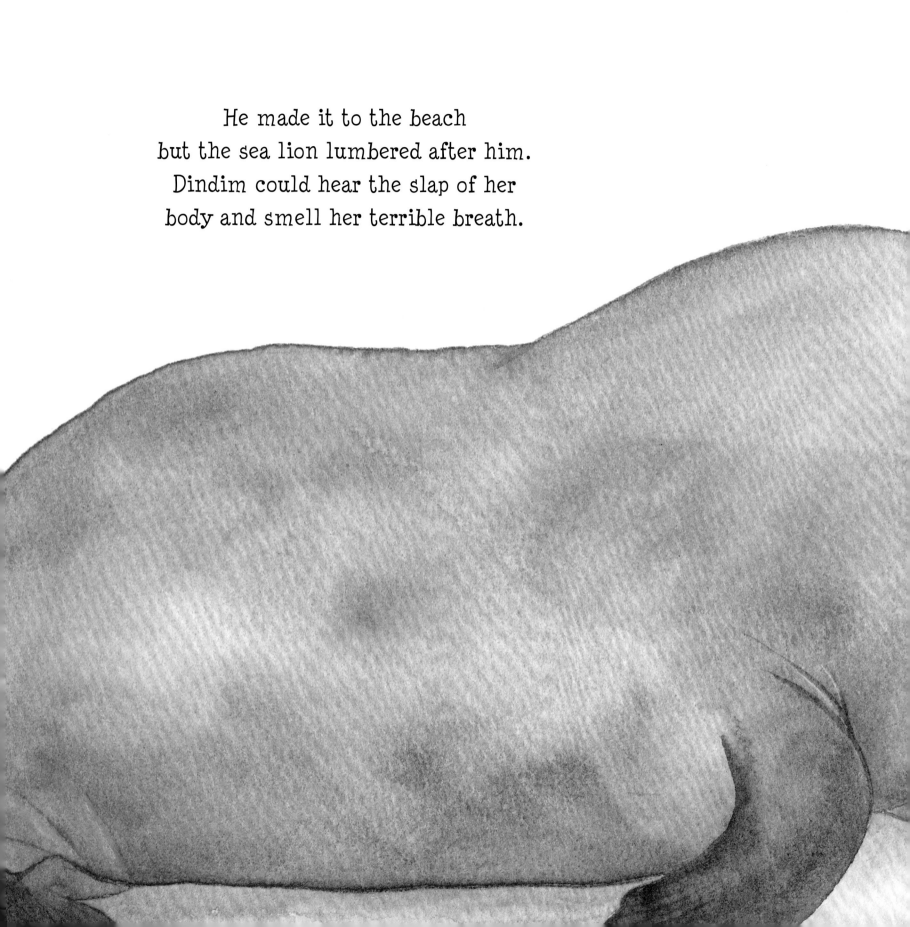

He pushed himself
harder, thinking only
of making it to Joao.
He was so close now.

Dindim squeezed himself through a
penguin-sized gap in Joao's fence, and was safe.

The sea lion slunk back to the ocean, defeated.

Joao was mending a fishing net. Dindim honked a
hello and wagged his fat little tail like a puppy dog.

Joao dropped the net and leapt to his feet.

As Joao bent to greet Dindim, he cried tears of joy. The penguin nuzzled his beak over the old man's face, chirruping softly.

Dindim curled into
the familiar shape of
Joao's lap, and sang his
lullaby of belonging.
He was home.

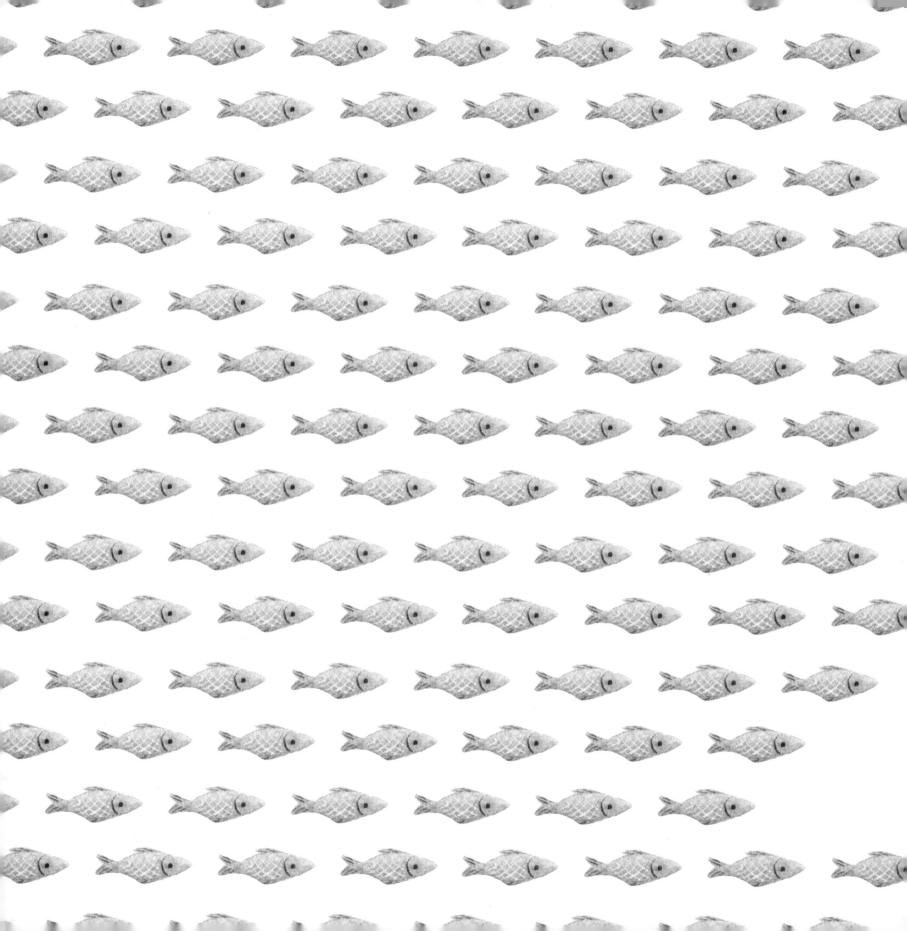